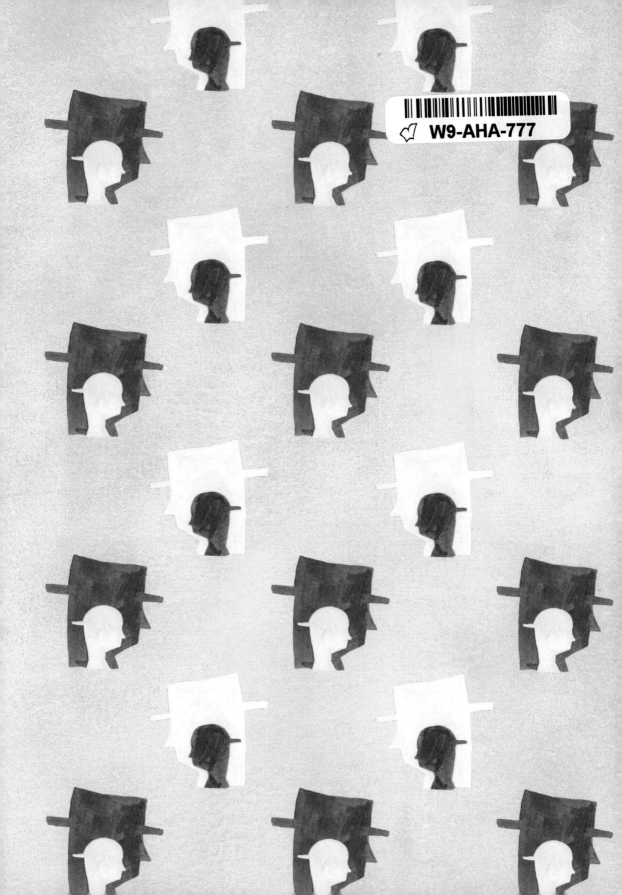

DEAR KIDS,

DID YOU KNOW THAT

ALL ADULTS HAVE A

CHILD INSIDE

THEM??

# ADULTS HIDE THEIR INNER CHILD BY PRETENDING TO BE BUSY AND STRESSED ALL THE TIME.

BUT AS YOU KNOW, IT IS IMPOSSIBLE..

TO KEEP KIDS HIDDEN.

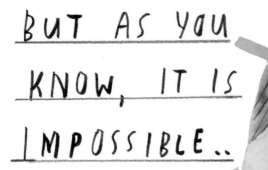

SOMETIMES AN
ADULT'S INNER
CHILD COMES
OUT
TO PLAY!

# COOL STUFF

USUALLY THEY CALL IT A GADGET OR SAY THAT IT IS SOMETHING THAT THEY REALLY NEED.

WHEN ADULTS
ARE
IN LOVE

THEY TALK

WITH

BABY VOICES

(GROSS!)

AND WEIRDLY,
THE OLDER ADULTS GET

# BEING A CHILD IS AN IMPORTANT TIME

YOU LEARN THINGS THAT YOU CAN NEVER FORGET.

WHEN YOU ARE OLD
YOU WILL STILL
HAVE A CHILD
INSIDE YOU.

IT CAN MAKE
THINGS HARD.

YOUR SISTER
WILL PROBABLY
STILL ANNOY
YOU.

AND YOU WILL
GET CROSS LIKE
YOU DO NOW.

WITH THE VERY
BEST WISHES,

HENRY

DEDICATED TO THE
INNER CHILDREN INSIDE
MY MUM & DAD.

**The Inner Child**
Written and illustrated by Henry Blackshaw

British Library Cataloguing-in-Publication Data.

A CIP record for this book is available from the
British Library.
ISBN: 978-1-908714-81-7

Published by:
Cicada Books Ltd
48 Burghley Road
London, NW5 1UE
www.cicadabooks.co.uk

Printed in China